By Elle Stephens
Based on a story by Ann Austin

 A GOLDEN BOOK • NEW YORK

BARBIE™ and associated trademarks and trade dress are owned by, and used under license from, Mattel.
©2022 Mattel.
www.barbie.com
Published in the United States by Golden Books, an imprint of Random House Children's Books, a division
of Penguin Random House LLC, 1745 Broadway, New York, NY 10019, and in Canada by Penguin Random
House Canada Limited, Toronto. Golden Books, A Golden Book, A Little Golden Book, the G colophon, and the
distinctive gold spine are registered trademarks of Penguin Random House LLC.
rhcbooks.com
ISBN 978-0-593-64472-0 (trade)
Printed in the United States of America
10 9 8 7 6 5 4 3 2 1

One afternoon, Malibu and her sisters, Skipper, Stacie, and Chelsea, were cleaning up trash from the ocean with their friend Brooklyn. Suddenly, a necklace in Malibu's bag started to glow!

A mermaid named Isla had given Malibu the necklace. The glowing necklace meant Isla needed help!

Malibu put the necklace around her neck and asked her sisters and Brooklyn if they would go with her.

Malibu's sisters and Brooklyn were ready to help! They all joined hands and jumped into the ocean together. Thanks to the necklace, they all turned into beautiful mermaids!

In the underwater kingdom of Pacifica, Isla was happy to see everyone. She explained that the mermaids were preparing for a Moon Ceremony to keep Pacifica safe. But it would only work with the powers of eight special mermaids, and two were missing.

Isla and the girls swam to the Great Arena.
There, the chosen mermaids were getting ready
to compete in games that would determine
who would become the
Power Keeper!

Just then, the mermaid queen, Coralia, announced that Malibu and Brooklyn were two of the chosen mermaids. And one of them might be the Power Keeper!

"In what world am I ready to do this?" Brooklyn asked nervously.

"This world!" said Malibu.

A young mermaid named Aquaryah offered to
help Malibu and Brooklyn practice the four powers:
air, water, earth, and fire.

"We really appreciate this, Aquaryah!" said Malibu.

"You're helping me, too!" said Aquaryah. "The more
I practice, the sooner I'll find my power."

While practicing, Brooklyn soon discovered that she was a fire mermaid. Stacie discovered she was an earth mermaid.

The day of the competition arrived, and Malibu and Brooklyn watched a merman named Finn gain his earth power. As they congratulated him, no one noticed a submarine lurking on the surface of the water above them.

Inside the submarine, a scientist named Marlo was determined to prove that mermaids were real. She had found a mermaid crown, and her anglerfish used the scent to find mermaids.

"Lead me to them!" Marlo called.

Back in Pacifica, Chelsea told Aquaryah that she could understand what a little whale name Viva was saying.

"Only a water mermaid can do that!" cried Aquaryah.

Chelsea was a water mermaid! She got a tiara, too.

The girls were so excited they didn't notice Marlo's anglerfish swimming toward them.

All of a sudden, two large nets swooped down
and trapped Chelsea and Aquaryah! The nets
pulled the mermaids up to Marlo's submarine.
Luckily, Viva swam away to get help.

Back at the competition, Malibu noticed that she was the only one who hadn't received her power yet.

"Don't worry," said Brooklyn. "You're the one who showed me that magic is real."

Just then, Viva arrived. She told them that Chelsea and Aquaryah were in trouble.

But that wasn't the only problem. Queen Coralia announced that an island of trash was moving toward Pacifica!

While the mermaids went to help the queen destroy the island of trash, Malibu quickly swam after Viva to save Chelsea and Aquaryah.

Malibu reached the submarine and took off her necklace to turn into a human. Marlo was surprised to see her and told her that Chelsea and Aquaryah had escaped.

The submarine hit something and began to flood! Malibu lost her necklace, and Marlo dropped the mermaid tiara.

As the submarine broke apart, Marlo needed help. Malibu saw her necklace and put it on the scientist. Marlo turned into a beautiful mermaid!

Suddenly, a piece of the submarine hit Malibu and pushed her toward the ocean floor!

Chelsea and Aquaryah tried to help, but Malibu was trapped . . . until the mermaid tiara floated down and landed on her head.

Malibu began to glow and turned into a mermaid. She was a water mermaid!

But there was no time to waste. Malibu and her friends joined the rest of the mermaids in destroying the island of trash.

"We need to defeat it together!" Brooklyn told everyone.

The mermaids all used their powers, but the island of trash kept moving closer.

Then Aquaryah sent a huge wave toward the island of trash. She had water power!

But she wasn't done. The other mermaids watched as Aquaryah used water, air, earth, and fire powers together to form a giant golden ray. The island of trash exploded in a burst of bubbles.

Aquaryah was the Power Keeper!

That night, the mermaids prepared for the Moon Ceremony. They even invited Marlo to join them.

Brooklyn asked Malibu how she had turned into a mermaid without her necklace.

"It was Marlo's tiara," explained Malibu. "Queen Coralia said it once belonged to a Power Keeper."

"I think it was more than that," said Brooklyn. "It was in you all along. You just had to find it."

"I did!" said Malibu. "Thanks to all my sisters . . . and that includes you."

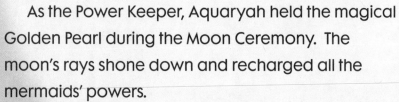

As the Power Keeper, Aquaryah held the magical Golden Pearl during the Moon Ceremony. The moon's rays shone down and recharged all the mermaids' powers.

Marlo promised to keep the mermaids a secret. And thanks to Malibu, Brooklyn, and their friends, the mermaids would be safe forever!